Mel Bay Presents

A Scottish Christmas for Fiddle

by Bonnie Rideout

**MUSIC FOR CHRISTMAS,
HOGMANAY,
AND THE NEW YEAR
AS PLAYED ON
THE FIDDLE**

CD CONTENTS

1	O Come, O Come Emmanuel/God Rest Ye Merry, Gentleman [4:14]	9	Baloo, Lammy [3:57]
2	Here We Come A-Wassailing/Bottom of the Punch Bowl [3:37]	10	Gloomy Winter [2:22]
3	Christmas Duanag/Hark the Bonny Christ Church Bells [3:00]	11	The Huntsman's Bag of Grain/Goosegirl's Song/New Year's Day [3:10]
4	What Child Is This? (Greensleeves) [5:42]	12	New Year's Day/On Christmas Night [3:26]
5	Rock Thee O' Child/Christ Child's Lullaby [4:31]	13	Yeoman's Carol/Sound of Sleat [5:13]
6	Christmas Carousing/Ale Is Dear/New Christmas [3:59]	14	Rorate (Nativity) [2:54]
7	Da' Day Dawis/Christmas Day I' Da Moornin' [4:20]	15	All Sons of Adam [1:55]
8	Adeste Fidelis (O Come All Ye Faithful) [2:53]	16	Auld Lang Syne [4:22]

**MAGGIE'S
MUSIC**

This book is available either by itself or packaged with a companion audio and/or video recording. If you have purchased the book only, you may wish to purchase the recordings separately. The publisher strongly recommends using a recording along with the text to assure accuracy of interpretation and make learning easier and more enjoyable.

Visit us on the Web at www.melbay.com — E-mail us at email@melbay.com

Official photo for the *National Geographic* "A Scottish Christmas" album release concert
performed at Grosvenor Auditorium, Washington, DC. Photo by Richard Crenshaw.

This book is dedicated to my husband

Jesus H. Medrano

For his love and support.

Merry Christmas

A Scottish Christmas at "The Stables." Bonnie Rideout has fond memories of Christmas on the Isle of Skye at Armadale Castle, home to the Clan Donald Centre, where she resided. Photo taken by the Executive Director, Rob McDonald Parker: 011 44 1471 844227 for research and visitation information.

Table of Contents

Acknowledgments

I would like to express many thanks to the musicians involved in the initial recording of *A Scottish Christmas*: Maggie Sansone, Al Petteway, Abby Newton, Eric Rigler, Charlie Pilzer and John Quigg. Thank you to Connie McKenna for helping with the text.... Geoff Wysham for his transcription, editing, and computer expertise.... Maggie Sansone and Richard Crenshaw for their team effort and vision.... John Purser for his suggestions and advice.... And to my family: Jesus, Adam, Clarice, and Molly for their endless patience, especially at Christmastide. *A Scottish Christmas* cover design: Graphic Images; cover photos: Dewitt Jones; Art Director: Richard Crenshaw; recorded at Bias Studios, Springfield, VA: Jim Robeson; digital mastering: David Glasser; Executive Producer: Maggie Sansone; Producer: Charlie Pilzer; Music Director: Bonnie Rideout.

HERE'S WHAT THEY'RE SAYING...... *A SCOTTISH CHRISTMAS - the recording:*

"The tempos are leisurely, the better to let the melodies ring; *the tone is pristine.*"

THE NEW YORK TIMES

"One of the best selling CD's of the season, the music is ancient and infectious."

CBS, "SUNDAY MORNING"

"Another splendid seasonal gift...reflective yet vibrant combinations of instruments in service to gorgeous melodies."

THE WASHINGTON POST

HERE'S WHAT THEY'RE SAYING...... *BONNIE RIDEOUT - the musician:*

"Her exceptional control when bowing, her ornamentation and her marvelously rich double-stopped drones produce an authentically moving, almost keening, sound."

THE SCOTSMAN, EDINBURGH

"...impeccable sense of intonation, timbre and phrasing with imagination....consistently enhanced by her impressive scholarship."

THE WASHINGTON POST

Introduction

Traditional music is best transmitted orally. With this in mind, I ask the reader of this book to understand that the black dots on the following pages represent only half the story. There is not one "proper" way of playing this music nor writing it down. The selections have been drawn from my recording, *A Scottish Christmas*. It would be impossible for me to write down all my bowings and every grace note, and yet these are important aspects of the music. Consequently, the recording provides an invaluable guide to one particular interpretation of these tunes. The chords accompanying the music are not necessarily representative of what each musician recorded, but rather are simplified versions designed to furnish an accompanying instrument a general chordal structure.

I encourage any serious student of Scottish fiddle music to listen to as many different traditional recordings as possible, not to mention making the journey to Scotland. In addition, it is important to keep your ears and mind open to the music performed on instruments such as pipes, harp, whistle, flute, and most importantly, the human voice.

About the Music

When selecting music for the recording *A Scottish Christmas*, I considered two important factors. First, since the project also featured the contemporary guitar style of Al Petteway and the "Christmasie" quality of Maggie Sansone's dulcimer, I needed to choose music that was conducive to their playing idioms as well as my own. Their unique sounds combined with the Scottish fiddle, pipes, and cello created a wide palette of textures to work with. Secondly, I chose a potpourri of repertoire to reflect the many moods of Christmas. Included are familiar Christmas melodies, lesser-known tunes from Scotland with seasonal titles, and a few choice classics that have nothing whatsoever to do with Christmas, but seemed too irresistible not to include.

Although the fiddle was not represented on every track, I have included the music with my arrangements, bowings, and harmonies. The tunes are listed by the order in which they appear on the recording for ease in playing along. I have also inserted some additional music which was not included on the final project due to playing-time restrictions on the recording.

This is by no means a complete collection of holiday tunes from Scotland, but merely an alternative to the general music associated with the season. Since there are several non-Christmas tunes represented in this collection, it is my hope that this book will not lie dormant for eleven months of the year with the reader's dusty collections of Christmas music, but remain with the rest of one's fiddle books to be enjoyed the whole year 'round.

Merry Christmas from the bottom of my punch bowl!

Biography

While searching for hidden Christmas presents in her mother's closet, Bonnie Rideout came upon a dusty, black, oblong cardboard box. The violin resting inside became her first love. That was 1970. Bonnie was eight years old.

Bonnie Elisabeth Rideout grew up on a "retired" farm in Michigan, but spent much of her childhood on an island in Casco Bay, Maine, where she studied in a one-room school house. "It was on Cliff Island where I learned the importance of playing by ear," she recalls. "Our teacher would gather all nine pupils and march us down the road playing the state song of Maine. My brother led the parade playing his trumpet, followed by the others on cymbals and drums, with me in the rear playing my violin. There was no possibility of reading music."

Bonnie's training in the oral tradition continued in Michigan, she says. "I scratched away on my fiddle while Mom played the piano and Dad tooted on his ocarinas. We played everything from 'The Moxie Song' to 'I Belong to Glasgow.' Playing by ear was so natural. It was at the heart of my most joyful music-making."

Bonnie received her formal violin training in Michigan. She played in public school orchestras and youth symphonies and took private violin instruction at the University of Michigan. She began college as a viola major but returned to the violin to finish her music and fine arts degrees in 1985. "I am indebted to the teachers who taught me the discipline of reading music and playing the works of the masters," she says. "But the more I played 'serious' music, the more I missed my fiddling." At the time she knew nothing of the folk world but had happy memories of music-making at home. It was the playing of renowned Scottish fiddler Dr. John Turner that opened a new world to her.

During the past ten years, Bonnie has immersed herself in the music of her ancestral Scotland. She has lived and worked in Scotland, fusing the traditions of her Scottish-American upbringing with those of the old country. She played with numerous strathspey and reel societies in Scotland and learned the different styles of fiddling from such greats as Ron Gonnella, Bill Hardie, and Angus Cameron. "Perhaps I was most influenced by an Aberdeenshire farmer, Jim Falconer (and his wife Katherine), who kindly took me into his home," she recalls. "Jim played the fiddle and spent many evenings by the fire coaching me and tearing away my 'classical' edges."

Her labors have made her a three-time U.S. National Scottish fiddle champion and brought her prizes in many fiddle competitions throughout North America and Europe. She is the first American to perform both the 18th-century and Highland styles of Scottish fiddling at the prestigious Edinburgh International Festival. She currently adjudicates, teaches, and performs on both sides of the Atlantic. In addition to her solo career, Bonnie is a mother of three. She resides with her family in Alexandria, Virginia.

Bonnie Rideout. Photo by Richard Crenshaw.

O Come, O Come Emmanuel

Traditional
arr. © Bonnie Rideout

Bb Pipe Tuning

God Rest Ye Merry, Gentlemen

Traditional
arr. © Bonnie Rideout

God Rest Ye Merry, Gentlemen

Traditional
arr. © Bonnie Rideout

Jig

Here We Come A-Wassailing

Traditional
arr. © Bonnie Rideout

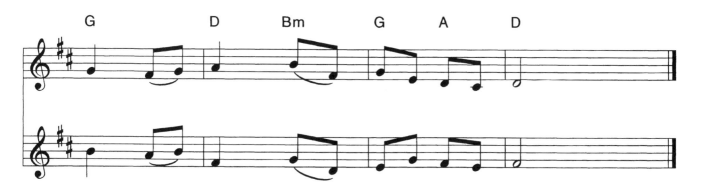

A Scottish Christmas at home in Michigan with Bonnie Rideout and family.
Left around the table: Clarice, Molly, Doug (Bonnie's Father), Bonnie, Adam,
and Betty (Bonnie's Mother). Photo by Bonnie's husband, Jesus Medrano.

Bottom of the Punch Bowl

Traditional
arr. © Bonnie Rideout

Bonnie with husband, Jesus Medrano, ready for a first
night celebration. Photo taken by Richard Crenshaw.

Duan Nollaig
(Christmas Duanag)

Traditional
arr. © Bonnie Rideout

Entrance to 15th century Rosslyn Chapel, Midlothian,
where Bonnie recorded "The Art of Robert Burns."

Hark the Bonny Christ Church Bells

Traditional
arr. © Bonnie Rideout

19

What Child is This?
(Greensleeves)

Traditional
arr. © Bonnie Rideout

Greensleeves

Snowfall behind Bonnie's home in Alexandria, Virginia.

Siud a Leinibh
(Rock Thee, O Child)

Traditional
arr. © Bonnie Rideout

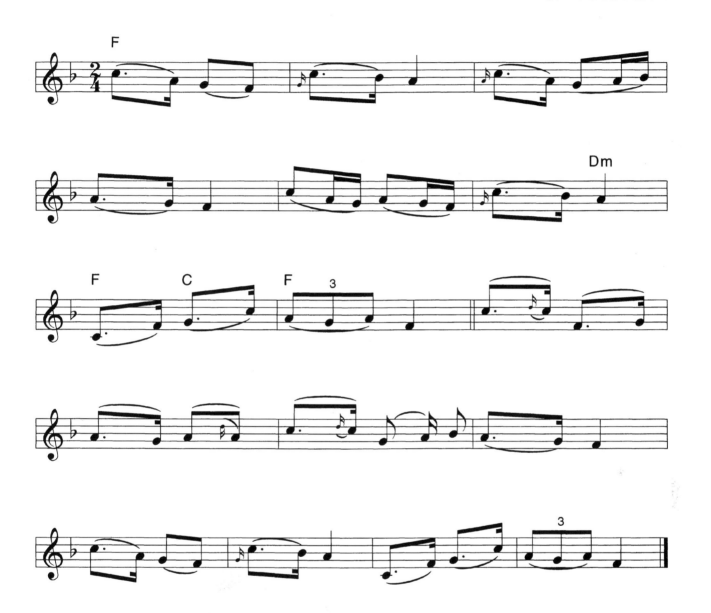

Tàladh Ar Slànair
(Our Savior Thee)

Traditional
arr. © Bonnie Rideout

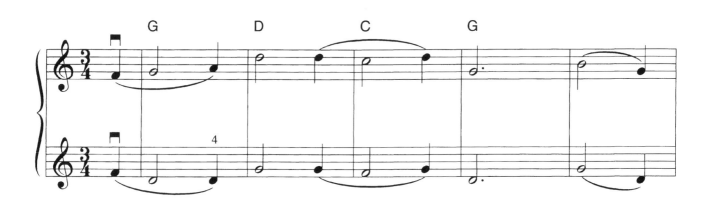

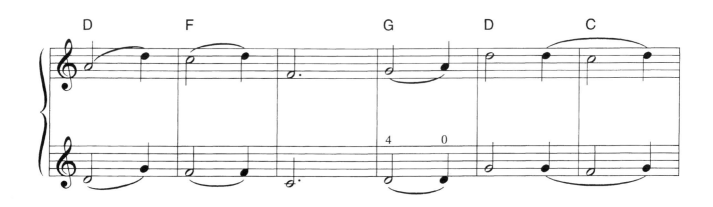

Tàladh Chriosta
(Christ Child Lullaby)

Traditional
arr. © Bonnie Rideout

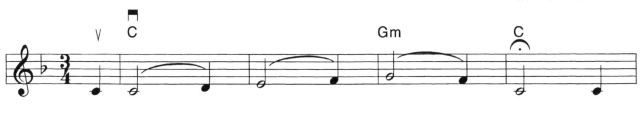

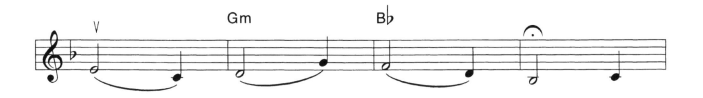

A Mhisg a Chur an Lolig Oirn
(Christmas Carousing)

Traditional
arr. © Bonnie Rideout
Strathspey

Christmas Carousing

Traditional
arr. © Bonnie Rideout
Reel

27

Ale is Dear

Traditional
arr. © Bonnie Rideout

28

New Christmas

Traditional
arr. © Bonnie Rideout

Da Day Dawis
(The Day Dawns)

Traditional
arr. © Bonnie Rideout

Slow

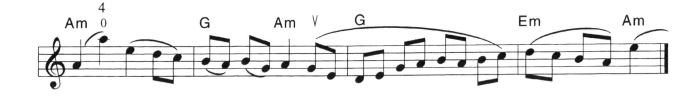

30

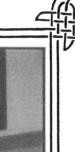

The "gang" at the *Avalon Theater* in Easton, Maryland during the Christmas '96 tour.
Left to right: Eric Rigler, Maggie Sansone, Bonnie Rideout, Abby Newton, and Al Petteway.

The "crew" during the video taping of "A Scottish Christmas, the Concert" for
CBS *Sunday Morning*. Left to right: Maggie Sansone, Dennis Jamison (cameraman),
Bonnie Rideout, and Bill Skane (Producer of *Sunday Morning*, CBS News).

Christmas Day I' Da Moornin'

Traditional
arr. © Bonnie Rideout

Adeste Fideles
(O Come, All Ye Faithful)

Traditional
arr. © Bonnie Rideout

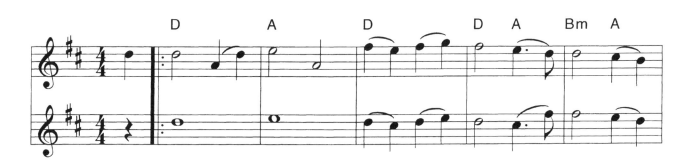

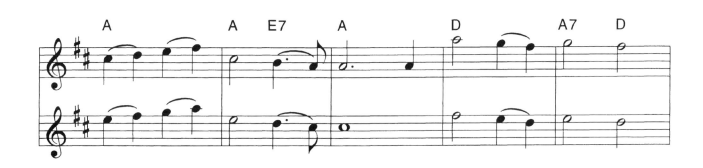

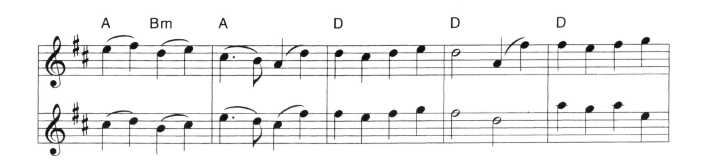

Baloo, Lammy

Traditional
arr. © Bonnie Rideout

Gloomy Winter

Traditional
arr. © Bonnie Rideout

Snowfall on Bonnie's back garden in Alexandria, Virginia.

Poca Sil An T-Sealgair
(The Huntsman's Bag of Grain)

Traditional
arr. © Bonnie Rideout

Gaasepigens Sang
(Goosegirl's Song)

Traditional
arr. © Bonnie Rideout

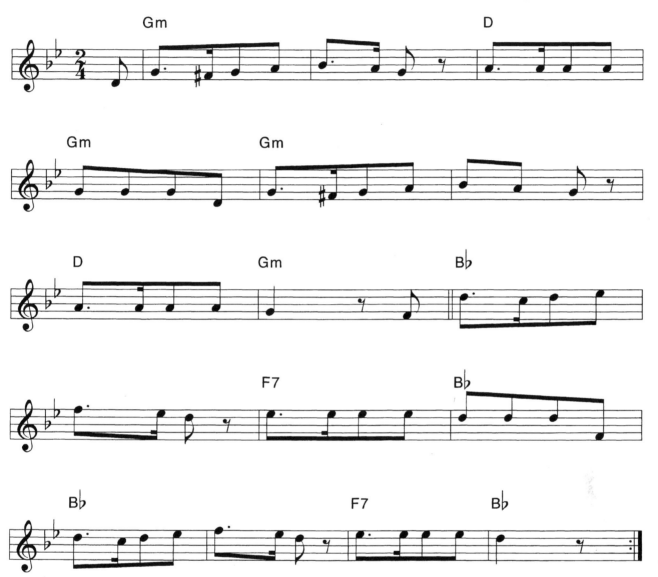

'Bhliadhn Ur
(New Year's Day)

Traditional
arr. © Bonnie Rideout

40

New Year's Day

Traditional
arr. © Bonnie Rideout

On Christmas Night

Traditional
arr. © Bonnie Rideout

Yeoman's Carol

Traditional
arr. © Bonnie Rideout

43

Sound of Sleat

Traditional
arr. © Bonnie Rideout

The Sound of Sleat. Looking west towards the mainland from Ardvasar, Isle of Skye.

Rorate
(Nativity)

Traditional
arr. © Bonnie Rideout

46

All Sons of Adam
(The Christmas Medley)

Traditional
arr. © Bonnie Rideout

48

Bonnie's son, **Adam** at three months. Born in Forfar, Scotland.
Photo taken during a Burn's Supper, 1988.

49

Auld Lang Syne

Traditional
arr. © Bonnie Rideout

A turn of the century postcard depiction; "Should Auld Acquaintance be Forgot."
From the Eudo Mason collection in the National Library of Scotland.

Christmas Round a 4 Voci

Traditional
arr. © Bonnie Rideout

Cheap Mutton

Traditional
arr. © Bonnie Rideout

Da Caald Nights O' Winter

Traditional
arr. © Bonnie Rideout

'Smairg A Chùrradh Spiocaire
(The Miser)

Traditional
arr. © Bonnie Rideout

Notes on the Music

O COME, O COME EMMANUEL (p. 10)
A 12th-century Latin carol.

GOD REST YE MERRY, GENTLEMAN (p. 11, 12)
A traditional Christmas carol. I composed the jig using elements of the original melody.

HERE WE COME A-WASSAILING (p. 14)
A popular Christmas carol throughout the British Isles. To *wassail* is to celebrate with drink, a common door-to-door activity often lost in modern neighborhoods, but still observed by my family whether our neighbors like it or not.

BOTTOM OF THE PUNCH BOWL (p. 16)
This tune first appeared in Oswald's 1742 collection of *Curious Scots Tunes*. It is commonly played for Scottish country dances around the globe.

CHRISTMAS DUANAG (DUAN NOLLAIG) (p. 18)
It was once more common in Scotland to use a method of chanting Christmas carols. This is one particular chant collected by Marjory Kennedy-Fraser as she heard it from Duncan Macinnes of Eriskay and in 1909 was published in Vol. I of her collection, *Songs of the Hebrides*. On Christmas Eve a group of men or boys (called goisearan or guisers), dressed in long white shirts and pointy caps, would go from house to house singing. After being admitted into the home, these Christmas lads (gillean Nollaig) would seek out a small child (or use a doll if necessary), place him on a white male lamb's skin and carry him three times around the fire. Songs of praise and offerings were then given to the symbolic baby Jesus. Before departing, the guisers would receive bannocks (similar to oatcakes), crowdies (a kind of soft cheese), or other treats before moving on to the next dwelling. The lyrics to this particular chant have an interesting Celtic-Christian theme when referring to the Christ Child:

> *"Son of Dawn, Son of Clouds,*
> *Son of Planets, Son of Stars,*
> *Son of Rovers, Son of Dew,*
> *Son of Welkin, Son of Sky."*

HARK THE BONNY CHRIST CHURCH BELLS (p. 19)
I came across this tune in a dusty corner of a used book shop in Glasgow. It was in an early 19th-century hymnal. Since the cover was missing, I do not know its origin. I later found the same melody arranged in a collection of vocal works "Selected and Arranged by *James Davie* and Respectfully Dedicated to all Catch & Glee Clubs - ABERDEEN." Although there was no date on this collection, James Davie was publishing music in the mid-19th century linking the eras of Gow and Marshall to J. Scott Skinner.

WHAT CHILD IS THIS? (GREENSLEEVES) (p. 20)
A 16th-century English tune. The final jig is a uniquely 18th-century Scottish version of this familiar melody which was originally entitled "Green Slievs and Pudding Pys." Unlike the slow version popularized by Vaughan Williams, it is a peppy jig often danced to by Scottish country dancers and having no association with Christmas.

ROCK THEE, O CHILD (SIUD A LEINIBH) (p. 23)
A Gaelic air collected from Mary Ross in 1900 on the Isle of Skye. It may originally have been a Norwegian lullaby and traveled with the Norse by sea down the west coast of Scotland. The lyrics to this beautiful melody translate to: *"Rock thee, O child! Rock to sleep, thou darling! Ere the birds begin to chirp thou wilt call. Thou wilt cry ere the cock will crow. Thou wilt cry ere the birds will sing. Rock thee."*

OUR SAVIOR THEE (TALADH AR SLANAIR) (p. 24)
This was originally a waulking song ("waulking" being a process for shrinking tweed cloth by hand) from South Uist. Catholics there adapted it for the church, singing all 29 verses during the Christmas Mass. It was first printed in the *Transactions of the Gaelic society of Inverness*, Vol.XV (1889).

CHRIST CHILD LULLABY (TALADH CHRIOSTA) (p. 25)
Similar to "Our Savior Thee"; a more familiar version of this popular Gaelic Christmas air.

A MHISG A CHUR AN LOLIG OIRN (CHRISTMAS CAROUSING) (p. 26, 27)
This tune is from the *Skye Collection* which was compiled by Keith Norman MacDonald and first published in 1887. The *Skye* book is a "must" for any Scottish fiddler's library.

ALE IS DEAR (p. 28)
A traditional reel and popular session tune for pipers and fiddlers alike.

NEW CHRISTMAS (p. 29)
This tune can be found in the *Skye* or *Gow* collections. "New Christmas" probably refers to centuries ago when the calendar changed and the holiday was moved to December 25th. Some Scots families also celebrate the "Old Christmas" in January.

DA DAY DAWIS (THE DAY DAWNS) (p. 30)
A popular tune from the Shetland Islands. Traditionally, a fiddler would play this tune from door to door to summon folk to church at sunrise on Christmas morning. It was John Purser who pointed out in his book, *Scotland's Music*, that this tune may have been popular during William Dunbar's time in the late 15th century. This melody has become a companion of mine throughout the year.

CHRISTMAS DAY I' DA MOORNIN' (p. 32)
A tune from the Shetland Isles, traditionally played after "Da Day Dawis."

ADESTE FIDELES (O COME, ALL YE FAITHFUL) (p. 34)
An 18th-century hymn.

BALOO, LAMMY (p. 35)
A 17th-century Christmas carol. "Baloo" is similar to using the word "hush" in a lullaby to soothe an infant to sleep. "Baloo, Lammy" basically means "hush little lamb," for:

> *"God's angels and shepherds, and kine in their stall*
> *And wise men and Virgin, Thy guardians all"*
> *...will keep watch over you...."Baloo, Lammy."*

GLOOMY WINTER (p. 36)
I learned this tune from my teacher at the one-room school I attended on Cliff Island, Maine. Miss VonTiling played the piano as we sang songs before class commenced every day. She pointed this tune out once, and I was attracted to its melancholy nature. The words to this tune actually speak more of Spring, but the title and its mood seemed to offer a nice texture to the *Scottish Christmas* recording, so we decided to include it. It is a love song.

POCA SIL AN T-SEALGAIR (THE HUNTSMAN'S BAG OF GRAIN) (p. 38)
This is a nursery tune from the Isle of Skye. It was collected and published in Vol. I of the *Journal of the English Folk Dance and Song Society*, 1932. The tune is very similar to the "Goosegirl's Song" which is Norwegian, although "Huntsman's" is set with Gaelic text and strathspey rhythms.

GAASEPIGENS SANG (GOOSEGIRL'S SONG) (p. 39)
A very old dance tune published in *Bornenes Musik*, Denmark.

'BHLIADHN UR (NEW YEAR'S DAY) (p. 46)
The *Captain Simon Fraser Collection* (1816) is the original source of this tune. Fraser mentions that he learned this tune from his father, so it could easily go back to the early 18th century, since Fraser was born in 1773. There are all kinds of strathspeys: lyric, gutsy, stately, quick, and undanceable (turn-of-the-century, virtuosi-type straths). I would call this a gutsy one!

NEW YEAR'S DAY (p. 40)
An 18th-century 6/8 jig by Gow.

ON CHRISTMAS NIGHT (p. 42)
This popular carol was collected by Ralph Vaughan Williams at Monk's Gate, Sussex, in 1904.

YEOMAN'S CAROL (p. 43)

A popular carol around the world. A *yeoman* was a person who owned and worked his own small parcel of land and was considered in a social class below the gentry. The word *carol* originally meant a circling dance, perhaps to symbolize the circular movements around the nativity crib that this dance emulated.

SOUND OF SLEAT (p. 44)

A popular pipe tune usually played as a quick march and often played as a reel by fiddlers. I prefer the slower "swingy" tempo that Maggie Sansone plays on her small pipes. She picked it up from Christopher Layer during a week stint at Hamish Moore's School for Cauld Wind Pipes. It was Maggie's favorite tune at the time of the Christmas recording, so we decided to medley it with the "Yeoman's Carol" because of the march-like feel they had together. The Sound of Sleat (pronounced "Slate") is a body of water off the Southern tip of the Isle of Skye. Near to where I lived during my residency at Armadale Castle, the Sound of Sleat is one of the most beautiful spots in Scotland. I used to go down to the water's edge at sunset and observe seals, otters, eagles, and all sorts of curious sea birds.

RORATE (NATIVITY) (p. 46)

This little-known Scottish melody is now popularly associated with Christmas. The verses were written by William Dunbar and set to the music just prior to the Reformation. The original Celtic-Christian appreciation of nature is prevalent in his inspirational lyrics. He begins with "*Sinner's be glad, and penance do.....Your souls with His blood to buy, and loose you of the fiend's arrest.*" He then continues with two extraordinary verses:

"*Celestial fowles in the air,*
Sing with your notes upon height,
In firthes and in forests fair
Be mirthful now at all your might;
For passed is your dully night;
Aurora has the cloudes pierced,
The sun is risen with gladsome light
ET NOBIS PUER NATUS EST.

"*Sing heaven imperial, most of height,*
Regions of air make harmony,
All fish in flood and fowl of flight
Be mirthful and make melody:
All GLORIA IN EXCELSIS cry
Heaven, earth, sea, man, bird, and beast;
He that is crowned above the sky
PRO NOBIS PUER NATUS EST.

ALL SONS OF ADAM (THE CHRISTMAS MEDLEY) (p. 47)

I was unaware of this wonderful choral work with the exception of a 13-bar segment in John Purser's book, *Scotland's Music* (Mainstream Publishing, Edinburgh, London). Having no access to the music on this side of the Atlantic, I was most grateful to receive a complete score from him in the post....with a quick humorous note which read: "*Well, you must somehow include ALL SONS OF ADAM. Without that you are all nothing!*" This medley of Christmas favorites contains "I Saw Three Ships" in perhaps its earliest version, which dates back to the courts of King James IV and V of Scotland.

AULD LANG SYNE (p. 50)

The music here is arranged with three versions of this popular song: the first with Allan Ramsey's 18th-century rendition, followed by an early Robert Burns version from the *Johnson Collection*, and ending with the song popular today, embraced in many countries around the world.

CHRISTMAS ROUND A 4 VOCI (p. 52)

This lovely piece of music was sent to me on a Christmas card from music scholar, Dr. David Johnson, author of *Scottish Fiddle Music in the 18th Century* (John Donald, Ltd., Edinburgh). On it he had typed:

> "Carol © David Johnson. Words by Martin Luther ('Vom Himmel hoch"), translated into Scots by the Wedderburn brothers, 1562. The carol is published under license by the Padagogische Forschungastelle der Freien Waldorfschulen, Stuttgart, in <u>We wish you a merry Christmas,</u> ed. Christoph Jaffke, 1984.

Unfortunately, we ran out of time on the recording for another fiddle "spot," although I have enjoyed performing it with ensembles ever since.

CHEAP MUTTON (p. 53)

An 18th-century strathspey by Nathaniel Gow. I like to play this tune as a "set" with "Da Caald Nights O' Winter" and "The Miser." Perhaps the mood sounds a bit "humbuggish" in title, but it makes for a smashing set of dance tunes and is appreciated at Christmas Ceilidh's by people like my father, who has annually sipped from his "humbug" coffee mug. He rather unceremoniously removes it from the cupboard each year in October when the first Christmas displays begin to appear in the shops....and does not put it away until the last piece of tinsel has vanished.

DA CAALD NIGHTS O' WINTER (p. 54)

A popular tune from Whalsay, Shetland. The music can also be found in a fantastic little book entitled *Da Mirrie Dancers, A book of Shetland fiddle tunes* edited by Tom Anderson and Tom Georgeson. This book was put out by the Shetland Folk Society and is loaded with great tunes and colorful local history.

'SMAIRG A CHIURRADH SPIOCAIRE (THE MISER) (p. 55)

A Gaelic reel I first heard at a session in Ardvaser, Skye. Ten years later I discovered its proper title in the *Skye Collection*.

Great Music at Your Fingertips

Made in the USA
Lexington, KY
14 October 2016